One Will Makes a Wish

On his ninth birthday, at his party, Will Seymour made a wish.

His birthday was on May the first, the day when spring starts growing into summer.

Will Seymour lived at number 3 Hawthorn Crescent.

The Crescent was quite unlike any other street in the town. It was the only one that curved. It curved like the new moon. Little cobbled paths ran between the houses, leading to wild, hilly fields where shallow, muddy ponds lay in the dips. And bang in the middle of the Crescent stood a hawthorn tree, heavy in spring with white, spicy-smelling flowers, heavy in autumn with bright red berries. It was a very old tree, so it was very large. Right at the top was an ancient pigeon's nest which hadn't seen an egg in it for years. On the day of

9

Will's birthday a white cat sat in that nest, watching everything.

Will lived with his mother, his father and his little sister Kezzie. His great friend, Owen Best, lived next door on one side and his great friend, Jack Dulac, lived next door on the other side. All they had to do when they wanted to play was climb over the garden walls. Kezzie's great friend was Lilah Price. She lived up the other end of the Crescent with her gran who kept a fruit stall.

On Will's ninth birthday Owen Best, Jack Dulac and Lilah Price came to his party. Owen brought him a flag he had made himself for the camp they had all finished building that morning at the bottom of the garden. Jack brought him a sword he had made himself with 'Will' painted on it in wobbly green letters. Lilah Price brought him a mango from her gran's fruit stall. He already had a watch from his mum and dad and a jar of frog-spawn from Kezzie. Will wasn't too pleased with the blobby frog-spawn, but all in all he was feeling very happy.

When they had stuffed themselves with

The Knights of
Hawthorn Crescent

On his ninth birthday Will Seymour
makes a wish – to meet magic. It is a
secret, but his sister Kezzie actually
sees it floating out in a bubble. Neither
Kezzie, nor any of their friends in the
Crescent can guess where Will's magic
will lead them. Not even when they
realise Miss Morgan is a witch and
that the hawthorn tree is full of
surprises . . .

Jenny Koralek
The Knights of
Hawthorn Crescent

Illustrated by John Lawrence

A Magnet Book

Also by Jenny Koralek
in Magnet Books

The Song of Roland Smith

First published in 1986
by Methuen Children's Books Ltd
This Magnet edition first published in 1988
by Methuen Children's Books Ltd
11 New Fetter Lane, London EC4P 4EE
Text copyright © 1986 Jenny Koralek
Illustrations copyright © 1986 John Lawrence
Printed in Great Britain by
Cox & Wyman Ltd, Reading

ISBN 0 416 10382 0

To P. L. Travers

Contents

little sausages on sticks and small, crisp chips, and chocolate biscuits, and tropical fruit salad sent up in a great bowl by old Mrs Price, Will was ready to make his wish. His father drew the curtains against the May sun. Kezzie jumped up and down. Owen Best and Jack Dulac crowded round. And then his mother brought the cake in, iced white with strong green spirals and bright with nine bobbing candle flames.

'Happy birthday to you,' sang his mother and everybody joined in. 'Happy birthday, dear Wi-ill, happy birthday to you.'

'Now cut the first slice and make your wish,' said his mother. She handed him a knife. 'And ssh everybody, ssh!' She laid a finger over Kezzie's lips. 'Not a word or the wish won't come true. Ready, Will?'

Am I ready? Will asked himself. Dare I? For he had a wish, of course, a wish long with him, ripe as an apple in autumn. Short in words but strong in force. If he made it, suppose it came true? Would he be happy or sad? Or both. How could he know now? He could not know now. His hand hovered over the cake. 'Nine to-day,' said

the bright icing. He looked round at the loving circle of his family, his friends.

'Ready,' said Will.

The room fell so quiet you could have heard a butterfly sneeze.

Will let the knife sink slowly, soundlessly through the soft cake and wished his strong short wish three silent times.

Then Kezzie said, 'What did you wish, Will?'

And Will said, 'You heard what Mum said.'

And Kezzie's eyes filled up with cross tears.

'I don't care,' she said. 'Anyway, I know what you wished.'

'How could you?' laughed Will.

'Because I'm your sister,' said Kezzie. 'Come on, Lilah,' she turned to her friend. 'Let's go and count my tadpoles.' And off she went, dragging Lilah by her sleeve.

'Don't mind her,' said Mrs Seymour to the boys. 'She's always crotchety when she's keeping tadpoles.'

'Why?' asked Owen Best, who was a great one for asking questions.

'She can't bear it when they turn into frogs,' said Mr Seymour,'and she has to put them back in the pond.'

'It always makes her cry,' said Mrs Seymour.

'Poor Kezzie,' said Jack Dulac.

'You've got a kind heart, Jack,' smiled Mrs Seymour. 'I'd better go and see if she's all right.'

'Now what shall we do?' said Owen Best.

'Finished building your camp?' asked Mr Seymour.

'Yes,' said Owen.

'Come and have a look,' said Will. He picked up Owen's flag. 'Let's go down and hang this up.' He waved the flag, which was made out of a white plastic shopping

bag nailed to a short mast and criss-crossed with red sticky tape. 'Follow me!' yelled Will. 'Follow my glorious banner!'

Mr Seymour, Jack and Owen trooped after him to the bottom of the garden. It was wildly overgrown and murky down there. The bushes were large and dark, lashed round with ivy, like frilly speckled snakes. The camp was well built out of old doors and also well hidden.

'Very nice,' said Mr Seymour, 'very nice indeed. Good idea that – covering it all with that old ivy.'

'We chopped a whole lot down with . . . er . . . with your little hatchet,' said Will.

'Oh you did, did you?' said Mr Seymour. He watched Will plant the flag over the camp's doorway. 'There now,' he said, 'just the job. I like it. I like it very much.'

'Well, Shady doesn't,' said Jack. 'Look!'

On the garden wall stood a huge drab-grey tomcat with narrow yellow eyes. No one in the Crescent liked Shady. He killed baby birds. Now his back was arched and his hair stood on end. He bared his little sharp fangs and drew in his breath with a back-to-front hiss.

'What's up with him?' said Owen.

'Well, whatever it is,' said Mr Seymour, 'he doesn't like your flag.'

'Don't suppose I'd like anything if I was Miss Morgan's cat,' said Will. 'If I was Miss Morgan's cat my hair would stand on end all the time. Skinny old spook. Never smiles, never . . . '

'Now, Will, that's no way to speak of a neighbour,' said his dad. Mr Seymour turned back to Owen. 'That's the George Cross you've got there,' he said.

'No,' said Owen. 'It's the Red Cross.'

'Red Cross, George Cross,' said Mr Seymour. 'What's the difference? It's not pirates, is it? It's not skull and cross-bones. I can sleep easy in my bed with a flag like that at the bottom of my garden. What made you think of a red cross?'

'Don't know really,' said Owen. 'I just did. I've seen it on telly. On ambulances and hospitals . . . in wars . . . '

'Ahh,' Mr Seymour nodded and turned back towards the house for another cup of tea, pulling up a weed here and there on his way.

'I've seen the red cross flag in a book about King Arthur and his knights,' said Jack Dulac.

'Knights,' Will echoed. He felt the word nudging his mind. He was back at the birthday table, daring to make his wish. 'Knights!' he said again. 'That's it!'

'That's what?' asked Owen Best.

But Jack, who was good at meeting

thoughts halfway said, 'You mean us, don't you? You mean *we* could be . . . '

'Knights,' said Will again.

All of a sudden the air went cold. As if the sun had gone behind a big black cloud. Will, Owen and Jack shivered, but each boy thought it was from excitement at the idea of a new, big game.

But there was no cloud across the sun. Shady was the cold cloud.

'Ice cream!' called Mrs Seymour from the back door. 'I'm sure you've got room left for ice cream before you go home.'

'And there's balloons!' yelled Kezzie. 'Come and get 'em before Lilah and me float right up to the ceiling.'

'We'll start the great new game first thing tomorrow,' said Will to Jack. Owen was already running on ahead, his eyes always bigger than his stomach. 'We'll make swords and help old ladies over the road,' said Jack.

'But not Miss Morgan,' said Will.

'Kids, though,' said Jack. 'And lost animals. Cats stuck in trees. . . '

'We'll be the Knights of Hawthorn Crescent. . . '

They disappeared into the house, all talking at once.

And Shady froze on the garden wall. Then he let out a short, unheard yowl, followed by a low and terrible growl and silently floated like cat-shaped mist down the side of the wall, scudded over the neat lawn next door and vanished. A dirty puff of smoke if ever there was one. No one saw him go, except the white cat, sitting in the pigeon's nest in the hawthorn tree, watching, watching everything.

Two By Midnight Moonlight

That night Will could not get to sleep. Was it just the huge tea and all those presents? Was it the camp and the great new game? Or was it his wish? He tossed, he turned and counted crowds of sheep.

A ray of moonlight began to fill the room with annoying brightness. And then the grandfather clock down in the hall struck one which meant it was midnight. The clock had been an hour fast ever since Kezzie had swung on the pendulum when she was three to try and make Christmas Day come sooner.

As the clock struck, the moon's ray reached Will's face. He jumped out of bed and ran to the window. The crescent looked beautiful and mysterious. Silver light lay across the curved rooftops as if the new moon had landed there. Silver light spilled across the road. Unmoving shadow lay in between. But all of a sudden a small piece of that shadow slunk into the shining road and broke into the shape of a cat. And then Will heard a voice.

'Shady,' it called, low, cold, sharp. 'Wait. Wait for me.'

Another piece of shadow broke into the light, a tall, upright shadow.

'Miss Morgan!' whispered Will. 'It's Miss Morgan.' And he went cold all over, there in his cosy room, just as he did whenever this strange neighbour passed him in the street.

Miss Morgan kept herself to herself over the road in a tall narrow house with blinds on all the windows. Her hair was white, but her face had no wrinkles – not like Grannie Price's at all – but somehow Will knew she was old, very old, even older than the hills. She often carried a stick carved with eyes. Her own eyes were very odd. One was green and one was brown. Mostly she kept them cast down but once or twice she had given Will a quick flickering look which had made his heart miss a beat. Her garden was paved all in stone except for nettles and dandelions in the mean cracks. She made soup from her nettles and salad from her dandelion leaves. Will had seen her grasping the nettles with no sign of pain and yanking up dandelions by the roots like a dentist pulling out a tooth. Although her hands were long, slender and delicate, like the hands of a princess, Will did wonder if their bones were made of iron. He'd never seen her teeth because she never spoke to him or smiled but he did wonder if they, too, were made of iron. Will steered clear of Miss Morgan. He feared her.

'Funny time to be going for a walk,' muttered Will. 'But then she's a funny person. Well, not a *funny* person – a very strange and horrid person. If I were Miss Morgan I'd feel happier at night with no one staring at me. And as for Shady. . . ugh! If I had a cat who killed baby birds, I'd be sneaking out at night when everyone else is asleep. . . '

'Will!' came a little voice behind him.

Will spun round.

'Kezzie!' he hissed. 'You gave me a real fright! What on earth are you doing here? You should be asleep.'

'The moon woke me up,' said Kezzie, 'so I got up and counted my tadpoles without turning on the light. There's twenty-three and no frogs!' She smiled up at Will. 'Then I heard you talking to yourself so I thought I'd come and see you. . . '

'I wasn't talking to myself,' said Will hotly. 'Keep quiet and come here. There's something very queer going on out there.'

Kezzie crept to the window. The tall shadow and the cat shadow were now circling the hawthorn tree.

'It's a witch!' whispered Kezzie. 'And a witch's cat. Look! She's even got a wand!'

'Don't be silly,' said Will. 'It's only Miss Morgan and that beastly Shady.'

'But she could be a witch,' argued Kezzie.

'No,' Will insisted. 'I know Miss Morgan's strange and scary but that's all she is – strange and scary, sometimes very scary. There's no such thing as witches any more.'

But even as he spoke the air round Will went as cold as if he'd stepped into a fridge. Miss Morgan began to sing. She pointed her stick at the tree and Shady's tail shot

23

up as if it had been electrified. Round and round the tree they went. At first all Kezzie and Will could hear was the ice in Miss Morgan's voice. Then the words became clear:

'You'll never get out, you'll never get out, you'll never get out, you'll see.
You'll never get out, you'll never get out, never get out of your hawthorn tree.
But if you got out, if you got out
You'd come face to face with MEEE. . . '

Three times backwards round the tree went Miss Morgan and her cat. Three times she sang her song to a menacing rhythm like an enemy drumbeat. Then, 'Come on, Shady,' she snapped. 'That should do the trick. Time for bed.' Then Will heard the clang of her teeth as she scooped Shady up in her arms and vanished into the black.

'Pinch me,' said Kezzie. She seemed more excited than afraid.

Will forced himself to stop staring on and on out into the night and sank a trembling finger and thumb into Kezzie's plump little arm.

'Ouch!' cried Kezzie. 'Well, it wasn't a dream, so it must be your wish. Oh Will, whatever have you done making that wish? I think it's coming true!'

Will gawped at her. He was rattled, thoroughly rattled. 'Never you mind about my wish,' he growled.

'But I do mind,' said Kezzie, 'specially as I seem to be in it now. Anyway, I saw it coming out of your head. Like a balloon with writing on it. "Let me meet magic." That's what it said, so there!'

'Well, you just keep your mouth shut,' Will said. 'I don't want everybody laughing at me. Now you go straight back to bed this minute. We're both half-asleep and imagining things. You know how weird Miss Morgan is. But if you tell *anyone* about tonight, or what I wished I'll . . . I'll . . . '

'Oh, I can keep a secret,' sniffed Kezzie. 'I've been keeping secrets for days and nights and weeks and years. In fact ever since I was born.' And she left the room with her head held high, like a great queen who has seen many strange things in many strange lands.

And now Will was tired, tired from top

to toe, inside and out. He fell like a stone on to his bed into deep, dark sleep.

Then, and only then, did the white cat in the pigeon's nest creep out and disappear into the heart of the hawthorn tree.

Three To the Rescue

Next morning Will's memory of the night was very dim. It had slipped into the place of dreams. The sun was up and when the sun is up it is very easy to forget the night. Besides, he could smell toast and bacon. Will's nose twitched and his mouth watered. He ran downstairs, hungry again and eager to be off with Owen and Jack making swords and getting ready to be knights.

Kezzie was already at the table, cradling her blobby frog-spawn jar and counting her tadpoles with her mouth full. She looked at Will. 'Twenty-five,' she said. 'And one's got two back legs,' she added sadly in her own usual voice.

'Well, you know it's got to happen,' said Will. 'They can't stay tadpoles for ever.' He made a bacon sandwich and headed for the door.

'Where are you going?' asked Kezzie. 'Or is it another secret?'

'You sound like a talking sour grape,' said Will. 'What's got into you? Of course it's not a secret. I'm going to play with Jack and Owen like we said yesterday.'

'Play what?'

'We're going to make swords and be knights.'

'You can't be knights without a king,' said Kezzie.

'I don't see why,' said Will.

'I do,' said Kezzie. She jumped up, frog-spawn and all, and followed him into the hall. 'I'm coming too,' she said.

Will could have kicked himself, but it was too late.

'It's not a girls' game,' said Will.

'I'm going to get Lilah,' said Kezzie.

'Girls can't have swords and be knights,' said Will.

'Well, Lilah and me can,' said Kezzie, hands on hips. 'If you don't let us,' she went on, 'I'll tell your secret.'

'What secret?' asked Will, brushing crumbs and bacon bits off his chin.

'You *know*,' nudged Kezzie. 'Last night.'

'Last night? What about last night?'

'The witch and the spell.'

'The witch and the spell?' As Will repeated the words the memory half slid out of the place of dreams. 'Ohhh! That! Miss Morgan and Shady being daft round the tree?'

'Mm,' said Kezzie. '*And* I'll tell your wish.'

Will felt as if he'd been stabbed. Now, by the light of day, any idea he'd had that Miss Morgan was a witch had faded away. But his *wish* was another matter. His wish had been with him for a long time, long before his birthday.

'Oh go on, then,' he said. 'Go and fetch Lilah. We'll be at the camp.'

Very carefully Kezzie put the frog-spawn jar down on the hall table and shot out of the front door straight up to Grannie Price's fruit stall. Everyone in the Crescent must have heard her yelling 'Lilah! Lilah!' all the way.

But now Will wasn't in such a hurry to join his friends. What would Jack and Owen say about Kezzie and Lilah wanting swords and being in the game? For a long,

30

long time he sat on the stairs tying and re-tying his shoelaces. He sighed, got up, ambled into the kitchen. Fed Jaws, the great fat goldfish. Took one bite out of an apple, shoved the rest in his pocket for later. Tried to pretend he couldn't re-member where he'd carefully put his sword the night before. Picked it up from the shelf right by the back door. Set off, very slowly, very grumpily, down the snaky, tree-filled garden path.

And all for nothing. Long before he reached the camp he could hear happy voices. Of course! Owen, with his eyes bigger than his stomach, was always nice to Lilah because she kept squishy fruits from Grandma Price's in a brown paper bag in her jacket pocket. And Jack? Come to think of it, Jack was always being nice to the little kids in the playground at school and had been sorry for Kezzie only yesterday about tadpoles turning into frogs.

Suddenly, not minding about the girls any more, suddenly glad about everything, Will stopped dawdling and pushed his way past the last large bushes into the camp.

There was Owen painting Lilah's name on a little sword. And there was Kezzie banging a nail into another little sword with Jack watching to see she didn't bash her fingers.

They all looked up when they saw Will.
'Hullo, Will,' said Jack.
'Where've you been?' said Owen.
'We've all got swords now,' said Lilah, offering bruised strawberries round.

'So now you're here,' said Kezzie, 'we can start the game.'

'Yes,' said Jack. 'It's your game. How do you want us to start?'

All four now crowded round him, swords at the ready, looking at him.

Will felt as if he had been crowned. And because he felt like a king, he behaved like a king. He raised his sword high in the air. The others did the same.

'Follow me,' he said. 'I don't know why, but I've got this feeling that if we go out into the Crescent *together*, *now*, the adventures will begin.'

Will was right. Before they were even half-way up the Crescent, a band of five, stretched across the pavement with Kezzie hopping, up-down, up-down, on and off the kerb, they came face to face with Mrs Rider. The Riders were a noisy, ferocious family. Everybody in the street was scared of one or other of them. Mr Rider was a postman. He was very tall, very broad and very strong with a bristly beard and eye-brows. Dogs never barked or bit Mr Rider on his rounds. Mrs Rider was pretty and bossy. She shouted at her children, but that

33

was brave because her twins, Gavin and Gary, were tough and rough. Their favourite game was tripping up little kids as they came out of the corner shop and running off with their sweets when they fell over. Then there was Lynnet, who was only three, but she was noisy too. When she cried she sounded like twenty baby starlings who hadn't been fed for a week.

'There you are!' cried Mrs Rider, as if she'd been expecting them. 'Our Lynnet's disappeared. I've been all over and I'm puffed out.' She seemed not to see their swords.

'Where are the twins?' asked Owen. 'Why aren't they looking out for her?'

'I packed them off on the bus,' puffed Mrs Rider, 'to wash their grandad's car. Keep them out of my hair for a bit.' She mopped her face. 'If you all fanned out and took a fresh look round . . . she can't be far off . . . little devil . . . ooh! . . . if her dad comes home for his dinner and finds her gone . . . I won't half cop it!' She clapped her hand to her mouth. 'Oooooh!' she screeched. 'The launderette! What if she's climbed into the tumbler . . . '

Mrs Rider started running back up the Crescent calling, 'Ooh, Lynn, ooh, you'll cop it, my love. Ooh! I'll cop it, heaven help us.'

Owen, Jack, Lilah and Kezzie turned to Will and stared.

'Do you really think she's in the tumbler?' whispered Owen.

'No,' said Will. 'She's probably where food is.' He fixed Owen with a knowing look.

'Sometimes she sits under my gran's stall with her doll.' said Lilah.

'She's got a new pram for that doll,' said Kezzie.

'Food . . . doll . . . pram . . . ' murmured Jack.

'Corner shop!' they all said at once.

'But that means she's crossed the road by herself!' cried Will. 'C'mon! Quick!'

Helter-skelter the five children charged into the main street, which marched up to the top of the Crescent, and dashed to the crossing. Then Will did something he'd always longed to do. Like a lollypop man or a policeman, he walked firmly out into the road with his sword arm raised. Car brakes slammed. Drivers shouted but all the cars slowed and stopped. The would-be knights flew after Will so fast they didn't hear. They whizzed into the corner shop which was old-fashioned and still sold millions of different kinds of sweets in huge glass jars and – there she was!

Lynnet, doll's pram and all, was standing on tiptoes holding out her few pennies,

demanding a liquorice bootlace in her starving starling voice.

'There you are, you naughty little girl,' cried Lilah. She swept Lynnet up in her arms. 'Your mum's worried sick. She thinks you've fallen into the tumbler.'

'I not in the *tumbler*,' said Lynnet proudly. 'I been shopping with Lady Di.'

'Well, now it's time to go home,' said Will, 'so give the lady your money, then you can have your liquorice lace.'

'Lady Di?' said Owen.

'That's her doll, silly,' said Kezzie.

Lynnet handed her money over to the corner shop lady, the lady handed over two liquorice laces. Lynnet clutched them in her hot, fat fist. '*No*,' she said to Lady Di, who lay grandly in her huge pram in a nest of frilly pillows, and blankets. 'You can't eat sweets before dinner.'

Jack seized the pram handle. 'Would you like a ride?' he asked. 'Shall we push you and Lady Di all the way home very, very fast?'

'Yes,' said Lynnet. 'Yes, yes, yes.' Lilah plonked her into the pram and Jack set off at ninety miles an hour. Will galloped

37

ahead, sword raised, but this time they
waited for the cars to stop for them before
Jack hurtled over the crossing. Lilah and
Kezzie cantered along on either side of the
pram. Owen brought up the rear. It was a
royal procession for a royal doll. Lynnet
loved it. She sat there laughing and licking
her liquorice. She had quite forgotten what

38

she'd just said to Lady Di. Her face grew blacker and stickier by the minute.

'Whoops! Sorry!' said Will as he almost knocked down an old lady who was standing at the kerb.

'Whoops! Sorry!' said Jack, quickly steering Lynnet and Lady Di round the old lady standing there with a large shopping basket.

'Sorry!' cried Lilah.

'Sorry!' cried Kezzie.

'Sorry!' giggled Lynnet.

But Owen said,'Can I help you? Can I carry your basket? It looks very heavy.' He put his hand on the handle. An iron claw shot out and clutched his wrist.

'Go away,' snapped the old woman in a voice as hard as hailstones. Owen froze. It was Miss Morgan and now she was staring at him. It was the stare of a witch working on a spell. Her eyes turned muddy and swirly like foul soup in a cauldron. They bulged like a toad's, then flickered like a snake's. Was she about to turn him into a beetle or a . . . SLUG? Owen felt a terrible coldness begin to creep up his body, first his feet, then his legs, then his knees. He grasped his sword. He was a knight. A knight never runs away. A knight shows no fear.

'Whatever have you got in there?' he asked.

With a shriek Miss Morgan tugged at the basket. 'Let go,' she snarled, tugging so hard that several tins of cat food fell out and began to roll this way and that.

'Look what you've done, you wretched boy!' screeched Miss Morgan. 'You've spilt my Shady's dinner. Pick it up! Go on! Pick it up at once!'

'Sorry,' spluttered Owen. He scrambled about in the gutter, stuffing the tins back into the basket.

'Now GO AWAY! Just GO AWAY!' growled Miss Morgan as he put the last tin back. 'I can MANAGE!' For a second she flickered at him like a flash of lightning and then she was gone, whether into the crowd or into thin air Owen never noticed. For Owen had seen deep into the basket. Tucked in among the tins of cat food, Owen had seen something which had nothing to do with cats' dinners, something shocking, something astonishing, something terrible.

He began to fly after the others, like a question-mark on wings.

Four Wizard Killer

'*Wizard Killer*?' said Will. 'Are you sure?'

Owen nodded.

'*Acid Rain*?' said Jack.

Again Owen nodded. 'Extra Strong. The Acid Rain said "Extra Strong".'

He'd caught up with the others just as they were handing Lynnet and Lady Di over to Mrs Rider. She had been far too busy scolding and kissing Lynnet to notice Owen's white face, or to hear him hiss out of the side of his mouth, 'Quick! Come to the camp! You'll never believe what I've just seen. Hurry, oh do hurry.' And now here they were, all sitting in a circle at his feet, not believing that he had seen "Wizard Killer" and "Extra Strong Acid Rain" in the bottom of Miss Morgan's shopping basket.

'What did they look like?' asked Lilah, cramming her mouth with cherries, forgetting for once to offer them round.

'They were in little bottles,' said Owen. 'The "Wizard Killer" was all . . . all oily and rainbowy, you know . . . like petrol in a puddle. And the "Acid Rain" was yellow . . . bright strong yellow but dirty at the same time . . . '

'She must be a witch,' said Lilah.

Will went very pale. Kezzie looked at her brother as if she could see his fighting thoughts. She pulled at a piece of grass, began to chew on it, but said nothing.

'But she can't be,' said Jack. 'There haven't been any witches for hundreds of years.'

'How can you be so sure?' snapped Owen. He had been half-scared to stone by Miss Morgan. Then on his way to find the others he had felt proud and important, and now here they were, all asking questions, but not the right ones.

'If you'd seen how she looked at me you'd believe she is a witch,' Owen said. 'Anyway, what I want to know is what's she going to do with that stuff? And why? And where? And *who to*? That's what I'd like to know: *who to*?'

Suddenly Will stood up. He stood up so

suddenly, so strongly, so strangely that Owen sat down.

Kezzie took the grass out of her mouth. 'Go on, Will,' she said. 'Tell them.'

'Tell us what?' said Owen.

'I've stirred something up,' Will stammered. 'I didn't know this would happen.'

'What do you mean?' asked Jack. 'What have you done?'

Will knew he must answer but it was hard, very hard for him to speak about a secret thing.

'That wish I made,' he faltered. 'On my birthday . . . '

'What on earth did you wish?' said Owen.

'To meet magic.' Will was near to tears. No one spoke.

'I – I don't think we're playing a game any more,' he went on. 'I don't know what Miss Morgan is up to, but I think I know where and when she's going to use that stuff. I don't know who she's going to use it on, but I believe now there is a "who", but I haven't a clue who the "who" is.'

Owen, Jack and Lilah stared up at Will.

What he'd just said sounded like gobbledygook, but he had spoken so seriously they, too, began to feel uneasy. Had they stumbled into another world?

Another world in their very own street, full of old, dangerous, powerful secrets?

'That's not all,' said Kezzie. 'Tell them what we saw.'

'No,' said Will wearily. '*You* tell them.'

'*We* saw?' echoed Owen. 'You mean you've both seen something and haven't told us?'

'Yes,' said Kezzie. She got up and stood beside Will. 'Last night we saw Miss Morgan putting a spell on the hawthorn tree.'

'Or rather, a spell on someone *in* the hawthorn tree,' said Will. 'Only I told Kezzie to keep her mouth shut because I was afraid you'd all think I was daft. Kezzie said at once Miss Morgan was a witch, but I told Kezzie she was silly. I wouldn't believe what I was seeing . . . Miss Morgan dancing backwards round the tree, like a jerky clock hand . . . '

'Going widdershins,' nodded Kezzie.

'*Widdershins*?' echoed Owen, 'What's widdershins?'

'Going round the wrong way,' said Kezzie. 'Like Rumpelstiltskin danced round his fire when he thought he'd won the queen's baby. Like witches stir cauldrons.'

'How do you know?' snapped Owen.

'I just do,' said Kezzie. 'So does Lilah, don't you, Lilah?'

47

'Yes,' said Lilah. She blew out a few cherrystones and wiped juice off her chin.

'*And* Will knows,' Kezzie went on happily. 'Well, Will doesn't know what I know, but he knows that *I* know what I know.'

'Oh shut up, Kezzie,' cried Will. 'Why don't you go and count your frog-spawn?'

'No,' said Jack Dulac. 'Not now. What else was Miss Morgan doing?'

'Waving her stick,' said Will.

'Wand,' said Kezzie.

'Wand,' said Will. 'And singing a nasty song.'

'What was she singing?' asked Owen.

'Something like "You'll never get out, you'll never get out," over and over again.'

'"And if you get out you'll come face to face with me",' added Kezzie. 'She said "me" in such a snarly voice that Shady yowled.'

'Sounds as if she was talking to someone she knows,' said Jack.

'A wizard,' said Lilah. Out flew a few more cherry stones. 'S'obvious. She's going to kill him. Like they do badgers. And then she'll do the tree with the Acid Rain . . . '

48

'Why?' said Owen.

'So another wizard won't come,' said Kezzie.

'Wizards like living in hawthorn trees,' said Lilah. 'My gran says.'

'Merlin went to sleep in a hawthorn tree,' said Kezzie.

'Merlin?' said Jack Dulac, eyes bright and keen like a dog on the scent.

'He went to sleep in a hawthorn tree for thousands of years, I know . . . '

'Yeah,' said Jack quickly. 'We know you know.'

'Poor wizard,' said Lilah in a wobbly voice. 'And if he *does* get out before the poison kills him then she'll turn him into stone, or into a frog . . . '

Kezzie winced.

'Or chase him round the world for ever and ever,' Lilah went on, 'and he'll never get away from her and never be able to have a nice kip.'

'We've got to do something,' said Will.

'Of course,' said Jack Dulac, leaping to his feet.

'But what?' asked Owen.

'Stand guard,' said Will. 'Watch that tree . . . '

'Tonight and every night till she comes with her poisons,' said Jack Dulac, 'and finds a ring of knights right round it.'

'And then what?' said Owen.

'We'll throw cabbage stalks at her,' said Lilah. 'And rotten tomatoes.'

'And squirt Shady with my water pistol,' said Owen. 'Cats hate getting wet.'

'And put up our swords,' said Will, raising his then and there. He lowered it again swiftly. 'I told you,' he urged 'it's not a game any more. If you think what Miss Morgan's like – and if she really is a witch, she's not any old sort of witch – she's a queen witch.' He sighed. 'It'll take more than we've got to fight her. Much more. We'd need magic of our own.'

'Perhaps it'll come,' said Jack, 'if we get out there and do the best we can.' Will smiled gratefully at his friend.

'But however will we get out there – at night?' said Owen. 'My mum can hear me turning a comic over through the floorboards . . . '

'We'll ask to sleep out,' Will announced, very much the king again. 'After all we've got our own camp now. Kezzie and Lilah can sleep in it and us three'll fit into Jack's tent . . . '

'They let us do it last summer,' said Jack. 'They'll just think we're having another midnight feast.'

'Yes!' cried Owen. 'That was great! Sneaking off to the baker's for doughnuts, and fizzy lemonade and them pretending all the time they didn't know what we were up to!'

'The main thing,' said Lilah, 'the main thing is, we'd better get plenty of food so they do think we're just having a midnight feast.'

'Of course,' agreed Will. 'They mustn't suspect for a minute what we're really up to. In fact, if we're going to start keeping watch tonight we'd better get things ready now.'

The other children scrambled to their feet.

'They were really nice last time,' said Jack. 'Didn't bother us at all.'

'But what if they do this time?' said Owen.

'They won't,' said Kezzie. 'I bet they had midnight feasts when they were little.'

'Young,' said Will. 'Not little. Young.'

'Young,' said Kezzie quite meekly for such a know-all.

Kezzie was right. The grown-ups were no trouble at all. The weather was warm for early May. It was Friday night so there was no school next day.

'Come on, you two,' whispered Will. 'We can't move till the lights go out in all our houses, so we might as well have the feast now.'

He did not add that his stomach had gone into such a knot of fear, the very thought of eating any food made him feel sick. He did not know, as they sprawled there in the dark that all his friends had knots of fear in their stomachs, even Owen, even Lilah. He took one small bite out of the squidgy doughnut and pushed the rest out of sight under the ivy. He did not see Kezzie and Lilah hide theirs in their rotten fruit bags. He did not see Jack and Owen bury theirs in the long grass. His mouth was strangely dry. He gulped down some lemonade and passed the bottle down the line. Everyone seemed glad of the drink, but there was no giggling, no burping. The pretence of feasting fizzled out like a damp firework and for a long time they just waited in silence for their parents to go to bed.

Five Night Flight

The children lay and watched the patterns of lighted windows shift in each house. They all felt a sudden need to talk, to hide fear behind words.

'Sitting-room light's out,' whispered Jack. 'That means the TV's off and the cat's been let out and in.'

'Our kitchen light's gone out,' said Will.

'That means they've finished their tea,' said Kezzie.

'Bedroom lights on everywhere now,' said Owen.

'And bathrooms,' said Jack. 'Teeth cleaning. Et cetera.'

'Landing lights off,' said Owen.

'Hope Mum doesn't brush her hair a hundred times tonight,' said Kezzie.

'And Dad doesn't read too long,' said Will.

'My mum and dad always go out like lights,' said Owen.

Silence drowned the joke and all the windows went dark.

'There they go,' said Jack. 'Tonight they've all gone out like lights.'

No one laughed.

Now the warm lights of home had gone out the real reason for being out in that garden in the middle of the night hit Will hard. But he mustn't show his friends he was scared. Besides, they must finish what they'd started.

'We'd better wait a few more minutes,' he said, 'and then . . . we can go.'

A different kind of light shone down now as the silver-cold light of the moon sailed out from behind one small cloud. Nobody spoke. Nobody moved. No sound came from their houses. They were on their own in a sleeping world.

'Ready,' whispered Will. 'Follow me. Down the alley. Single file. Jack first, then you girls. Owen bring up the rear. No talking and feet like cats' paws! Don't forget your swords and the mouldy tomatoes and remember: we must wait till midnight. Last time she came at midnight.'

The others obeyed. Glad to have a leader. Glad to be on the move.

Looking over their shoulders every few seconds, keeping to the shadowy hedges of the Crescent, they reached the hawthorn tree like shy ghosts.

'Now what?' said Owen. He stared up at the tree's twisted, narrow branches, the thorny twigs hidden by the blossom and thousands of small leaves. 'How are we going to hide?'

'It's not an easy tree to climb,' Will agreed. 'Not like an oak. But if we all make a circle round the trunk she won't be able to get through.'

'Kezzie and Lilah, you'd better stand between us,' said Jack Dulac.

'No,' said Kezzie, 'Lilah and me'll go round the other side. We're not afraid of silly old Miss Morgan.'

'Nuts in May,' said Lilah rather rudely and, giggling softly, the two little girls disappeared round the back of the tree.

For a long time they all stood there, backs pressed against the scratchy wood, hidden by the drooping leaves, gripping their ridiculous swords. Wide rays of moonlight lit the road, edged with black, uneven shadows. Shadows that might not just be shadows but evil watchers, enemies.

'It looks all different at night,' whispered Lilah. 'All strange.'

'Like my bedroom does when I wake up from a bad dream,' said Kezzie.

'Ssh!' hissed Will.

'What was that noise?' said Owen.

'What noise?' said Jack.

'It came from up there.' Owen pointed. 'Up in the tree . . . a sort of rustling.'

'Probably an owl in that old nest,' said Jack. They all peered upwards. He was right, but it was no ordinary owl. It was a white cat half-way through changing into an owl.

'Oh, stop making such a din,' said Will. 'Miss Morgan could arrive on roller skates and you wouldn't hear her coming.'

Again they settled themselves against the tree. They fell so quiet, so still, that they all heard the Seymour's clock strike one, which meant it was midnight. They all heard a breeze or a sigh shiver through the tree. They all saw pieces of the black

57

shadow break into shapes in the moonlight. A cat shape and a tall upright figure. Miss Morgan was moving straight towards them, but Shady stopped in his tracks. He pricked up his ears. He sniffed the air. His fur stood on end. His tail twitched violently.

'You little sillies,' said Miss Morgan. She spoke with a haughty, frost-edged sneer. 'Babies. Yes, I can see you too, Kezzie and Lilah. You don't really think you can stop me, do you?'

Shady growled deep in the back of his throat.

'Stop that, you wretched cat,' Miss Morgan commanded. Her eyes passed through and beyond the children to the tree. She raised her wand and began to shake the gleaming bottle she held in her other hand. 'It's all in here. My mixture. Nothing can stop me now.' And she began to speak a spell that splintered the silvery air like a cracking ice floe.

'You're going to die, old enemy, you and your tree. I've got the sword. Only I know where it is. Only I shall have it. It's too late now to help your precious master. Yes,

your master and his precious wife. I too, old enemy, can turn myself into the East wind and blast through doors and windows. I too can use the sleep of death

spell. And I did. And while they slept –
your master and his precious wife – I took
it. Yes! I took it. Oh yes, I too can turn my
nails into magnets and make a sword fly
through the air. The power's mine now,
old enemy, old fool. These babies can't
help you. You are going to die.'

Icy and cruel, her words fell on the
children like hailstones. Then the stare she
had fixed beyond them to the tree and
whoever was in the tree was turned on the
five cowering children.

'Be off with you.' She pointed her wand. 'Be
off before I turn you all into one-legged
giraffes with short necks, or changelings
whose parents won't want you any more,
or hairless polar bears, or frogs that can't
hop . . . '

Kezzie shuddered. And Miss Morgan
began to undo the stopper on her bottle.

'Don't move! Don't move an inch!'
hissed Will, barely able to force the fear-
weighted words past his lips.

The children couldn't have moved.
Although they shivered and trembled like
hollow reeds on a windy river bank, their
feet had turned to lead like they do in

dreams when tickling monsters are after you and your mother hasn't heard you calling.

'Don't be afraid,' said Will. 'Hold on to your swords and lean hard against the tree. Help is coming. I can feel it. It's coming from the tree.'

'I'm not afraid,' said Jack Dulac.

'Nor me,' said Kezzie.

'Nor me,' said Lilah.

'Why aren't we afraid?' said Owen.

The answer came in a flash like a thunderbolt. The ground shook. The tree began to shake, the branches to sway. A huge owl swooped down and seized Miss Morgan in its talons. The children's feet came unstuck. They felt themselves being pulled away from the tree and lifted upwards. Their arms began to flap like huge wings. Their feet were tufted and taloned. They were owls. They had turned into five small, strong owls.

The great owl hovered in the air. Miss Morgan was now squeaking like a mouse.

'Will, get the cat,' boomed the great owl, 'and then all follow me.'

Will found he could swoop as if he'd

always been a bird of prey. He seized poor bristling Shady in his talons and wheeled away with Jack and Owen, Kezzie and Lilah, all following the great owl's flight.

They flew down the Crescent, silvered as if the new moon had come to land on its rooftops. They flew over their houses, over their camp, over Grannie Price's fruit-stall, and the Riders' house where Lynnet and Lady Di lay safely sleeping. On they flew, on and on, over the wild hilly fields, over a house they had never seen before, a house with turrets and towers that shimmered and floated as if it was not grounded in the earth, until they came to three large ponds lying in the dips. And when they came to the largest, blackest pond the great owl dropped Miss Morgan right into it, ducked her into the shallow, muddy, freezing water. Proud to the last, she made no sound.

'Drop the cat too, Will,' said the great owl, 'then lead me to your camp.'

As soon as they landed on the dewy grass in the Seymour's garden they became themselves again: they became Will, Jack, Owen, Kezzie and Lilah, chilly and bewildered. Yet they knew then and they knew for ever that it had not been a dream. They had been owls. They had flown and they had given a nasty witch and her cat a ducking.

The great owl, too, had vanished, but there, sitting in the entrance to their camp, just beneath the flag, was a man. His hair was white, his beard was white, but his back was straight as an arrow. He was wrapped in a fabulous feathered cloak, held together more with stars than stitches, real stars that dazzled and twinkled like the man's eyes.

'You woke me up,' he said. 'But it had to be.' He looked at Will. 'A birthday on May Day, a ninth birthday on May Day, and your wish. I was bound to wake up. Well, I'd had a good long sleep – a thousand years or more. I was getting very stiff in that stuffy tree, so I changed myself into a cat and basked aloft in that old nest and saw things. Something very strange is going on here, or hereabouts if old Morgan's up to her tricks . . . .'

'Old Morgan?' said Owen.

'Morgan le Fay, boy,' said Merlin. 'A queen and a witch. A queen among witches . . . '

'Who *are* you?' asked Owen.
'Merlin,' said Kezzie and Lilah.
'Merlin?' gasped the three boys.

'Merlin.' The great wizard stood up. 'And now I must go and find the king.'

'The king?' said Owen.

'The king,' agreed Merlin. 'He can't be far off. He's in great trouble if she's taken the sword. She's been after it for many and many a year. Jealous from top to toe, inside and out. The world will be a sorry place if she holds on to Excalibur.'

'Ex-cali-bur?' stammered Will.

'The king's sword and only the king's. The power of Excalibur devours evil in the hands of the good . . . '

'And – and good in the hands of the evil?' said Jack.

'Precisely,' said Merlin. He swirled his starlit cloak about him. 'No more questions. I must leave you at once, but you will be sent for. That I can promise.' He smiled at their downcast faces. 'You will be sent for. But now Morgan's cruel cold shall melt. I changed her poisons into strength for me and morning dew for the earth. Sleep, my children, sleep.'

And sleep they did, soothed by Merlin's magic warmth.

Six The Messenger

A different warmth woke Will quite late next morning: the warmth of the sun. Then he heard his mother calling.

'Come on, you lazy lot! Up you get! Breakfast's ready and I need you to go shopping for Miss Morgan.'

Will sat up, completely wide awake. Every single thing that had happened in the night flashed before his eyes as if he had a film in his head. So Miss Morgan was back, was she? But what was up with her if she couldn't do her own shopping? And Merlin? Where was he now? And the king? Where was the king? What king? What king, indeed! If Merlin was about, and if Morgan le Fay had stolen Excalibur the only king it could possibly be was . . . King Arthur. But he hadn't fallen asleep for a thousand years like Merlin. He'd been killed in a great battle, hadn't he? Or had he? No, it was all coming back to Will. King Arthur had been wounded, not killed, and carried away by three queens in a great black boat. He was often called "the once and future king", so of course he wasn't dead.

Will looked at his sleeping friends, leaned over and prodded them. 'Hey,' he said, 'wake up you two. I've got to go shopping for Miss Morgan.'

'B . . . but Miss Morgan's in the pond,' said Owen, rubbing his eyes.

'Well, she *was* in the pond,' agreed Jack, crawling neatly out of his sleeping-bag, 'but she could easily have got out and walked home.'

Kezzie and Lilah, who had been awake for ages, were coming up the garden.

'Guess what,' said Lilah, 'Miss Morgan's got a terrible cold.'

Kezzie lagged behind, peering sadly into her frog-spawn jar.

'And we know why, don't we?' Lilah went on.

'So we do all remember,' smiled Will.

'Of course we all remember,' snapped Kezzie. 'It was only last night.'

Nobody snapped back. They could all see lively tadpoles jerking about in Kezzie's jar as if they couldn't wait to turn into frogs and get into the big wide world of the pond.

'What I want to know,' said Owen, 'is what we're supposed to do next.'

Suddenly the gap between last night and this morning seemed very wide indeed.

'Don't forget,' said Will, 'Merlin did promise we'd be sent for.'

'Let's have breakfast,' said Jack. 'We'll be able to think better after we've eaten. But we'd better not tell the grown-ups what happened last night. They'd never believe us.'

Another shout from Mrs Seymour brought them all to their feet and sent them running to the house.

'Well, you've had your beauty sleep and no mistake,' said Mrs Seymour. She plonked a plateful of bacon down on the table and a stack of toast. 'Help yourselves and get a move on, Will. You can wash up later. Miss Morgan's come down overnight with a dreadful cold. Funny, really, the weather being so warm and all. She's had to put herself to bed. She's in ever such a bad mood and in such a state about that cat of hers . . . '

'Why?' said Owen.

'He's taken a chill too and he's off his food. She wants me to get him some haddock. Haddock, I ask you! On a Sunday! Frozen coley more like. From the corner shop. Talk about royal treatment! She wants me to boil it up in milk, mash it, make sure there aren't any bones and I don't know what all. I'm rushed off my feet as it is.'

'Don't worry, Mum,' said Will. 'Give us the money and we'll go and get the fish.'

But they never got to the corner shop. Halfway up the Crescent they spotted Shady after his own breakfast. Haunches raised, crouched for the kill, his tail curled like a snake about to strike, his eyes narrowed on two white doves.

'They're flying straight towards him!' cried Will in horror.

'Can't they see him?' asked Owen. Kezzie nodded and bit into her thumb. Will looked quickly at his sister. Now what did she know that they didn't know?

'Shoo, you beastly cat,' sobbed Lilah. She lunged at the cat, who took no more notice of her than an elephant would of a midge. 'Go on! Scram! Go home! Shoo!'

But Shady took no notice, no notice at all. If an Alsatian had come after him at that moment he wouldn't have moved. He was hungry, he was angry, perhaps even under a spell. He was out to kill. And on came the birds so steady and so beautiful.

'Oh stop him! Somebody stop him!' Lilah covered her eyes and began to cry.

'They look as if they're flying that low on purpose,' said Jack.

The children watched in dumb sorrow as the birds drew nearer and nearer.

'They know what they're doing,' said Kezzie. 'They know.'

She was right. They must have smelt the cat, sensed the cat, but they made no sound of fear, no warning signal. They just flew straight on, one dove dropping ever lower and lower like a plane coming in to land.

'They're asking for it,' groaned Will. And as he spoke Shady pounced. In one perfect leap, his jaws half open he made a slobbery sound of snarling glee and he pounced. He moved so fast it was hard to see what happened. The dove's wings fluttered, once, twice, then fell still. Shady shook the bird between his teeth and began to maul it and play with it.

'No!' yelled Will running forward. 'Stop it, Shady!'

'Why are there so many cruel things?' asked Owen. 'Oh, I could *kick* you, Shady, but it wouldn't make it any better.'

Lilah was still crying, but Kezzie stood silently, holding on tight to her tadpole jar, biting her thumb.

Jack overtook Will, seized the dove and cradled it in his hand. Its wings lay, half-open like little broken fans. Will raised his sword over Shady. 'Go home,' he ordered. 'Go home before I hit you.' Shady growled, then cowered, then slunk away.

'And you won't find any nice haddock for your dinner,' Lilah shouted after him. 'We're not going shopping for you!'

'No we are not,' said Will.

'The other dove hasn't gone away,' said Kezzie.

They all looked up. With cooing sobs the other dove began to circle Jack who stood stroking the wounded bird.

'It wants to stay with its mate,' said Kezzie.

'What shall we do?' asked Owen.

'Take it home, of course,' said Kezzie.

'Home?' said Owen.

'Yes,' said Kezzie. 'To Merlin. They've come from him, I'm sure. If we start walking I bet that dove will take us to him and Merlin will make the hurt one better.'

'What a way to make sure we'd come!' cried Jack angrily.

'Let's do what Kezzie says,' said Will quietly. He put his arm round his sister briefly. Did she have some magic of her own?

Slowly Jack started walking on up the Crescent. But then the dove grew frantic. It began to flap its wings and fly a little higher.

'Am I going the wrong way?' said Jack. The dove cooed and wheeled round. The

73

children turned and followed it back the way they had come. Past Miss Morgan's, past their own houses, up the last little cobbled path that led to the wild, hilly fields. They often stumbled, not daring to take their eyes off the dove who flew on and on. It seemed to know the ways of wingless creatures. It kept to the tracks in the dips, guided them past the three black ponds. The journey, which had taken no time by night flight, was long and so slow on foot. All five children were flagging, Kezzie most of all with her heavy jar, when the dove led them through open, broken gates and there before them lay the strange house they had seen last night from the air. Even in daylight it did not seem to be grounded, as their houses were, in the solid earth. It *did* shimmer. It *did* float, as if it could take off at any time to some other place. The dove flew straight towards its great front door, which began to open as if they were all expected.

The children did not hesitate. They knew now without a shadow of a doubt that they were part of an unending story; that they had met magic in their own

street, in their own time. Only last night they had grown wings and flown. They had seen a real witch, a royal witch. They had seen her take a ducking. They had spoken with a wizard and now they had been guided to this house by a lovely, caring bird. So on they went, fearless, into the house, down dim passage-ways this way and that, always following the bird's white light, till they came to another door, which opened before them as the first had done, and they found themselves face to face with a king: the once and future king: here, now, again, his queen beside him, arms outstretched in welcome; behind them both, dazzling in the shadows, Merlin in his starry cloak.

The dove came to rest on the wizard's shoulder and Will led the children through the doorway. He knew at once – they all knew at once – that here was true magic. In the presence of a true king and a true queen they didn't have to put on any masks. So Will, as a small king before a great king, bowed. Jack held out the broken bird for Merlin to heal. Kezzie and Lilah ran to the queen and leaned against her because she seemed like a mother waiting to hug you after a long day at school. And Owen? Owen asked a question.

Seven This Day's Magic

'Can we help you?' asked Owen.

The king smiled and the queen smiled.

'Can you help us?' said the king. 'Look around you – all of you. Can't you see . . . '

'We've been waiting for you,' put in the queen.

The children stared about them.

The room was magnificent. Tapestries of rose and green hung from the walls. Life-like lions prowled through the woven thickets and unicorns peeped shyly from behind the trees. Faded banners hung from the ceiling with names faintly showing, names Will had heard in stories at bed-time: Lancelot, Percival, Galahad and many more besides. At one end of the room stood a great round table. At the other end a large bare stone.

Will's eyes lit up when he saw the table. He knew what that was. But it was the

stone, first and foremost, which drew his eyes back like a magnet again and again. There was a deep slit in it, but the slit was empty. 'The sword in the stone,' murmered Will. 'The stone but no sword.' He raised his eyes to the king. 'She took it from there? *Your* sword? From *your* stone? But you are the only person who can pull it out?'

'*Was* the only person, it seems,' said the king bitterly.

'She said she had nails like magnets,' Jack reminded them.

'And I know she's got iron wrists,' added Will.

'She's had a long time to strengthen all her powers,' sighed Merlin. 'A thousand years of my sleep. From now on I'll only sleep between sunrise and moonrise like all wizards, all witches.'

'Except at Hallowe'en,' warned Owen.

'Except at Hallowe'en,' agreed Merlin.

'She always hated knights,' said the queen.

'Shady must have told her about us,' said Kezzie. 'He was on the wall when we decided to be knights.'

'On May Day, too,' said Merlin. 'She'd have had her wits at their sharpest on May Day. Anything can happen on May Day.'

'Is that why I saw Will's wish float out of his head?' said Kezzie.

'I dare say.'

'Then I expect she saw it too,' said Kezzie.

'I dare say,' agreed Merlin, 'and why she sensed me stirring in my sleep. There!' he added. 'Look!' The broken dove, coaxed by Merlin's stroking hand, had woken out of its sleep of death and joined its mate. Merlin opened a little bubbly-green window and the birds flew out. 'Away with you!' called Merlin.

'Seek out other children in other crescents – and in the straight streets too! Children who want to be knights. Tell them you don't need armour and a horse to be a knight, but a brave heart and a nose for adventure. Tell them they have a king who was, and is, and will be, a king who comes and goes between the worlds. Tell them the world needs knights. Always has. Always will. See, Arthur, we have five here already.'

The king and queen seated themselves at the round table in two tall crowned thrones.

'Come, my knights,' said the king. 'Take your places with us and we will make a plan.'

The children saw then their very own names flickering like golden flames on the five chairs circling the table: Will, Jack, Owen, Kezzie, Lilah. Solemnly they sat down.

'But why hasn't Merlin got a chair?' said Owen.

'What need I with a chair?' said Merlin. 'I come, I go. I roam. I hide. I spy. I turn into this. I turn into that, and now, after all that sleep the last thing I need is to sit down. It's for kings and queens and knights to plan things. Planning is not my way. But give me your tadpoles, Kezzie. I'll hold them while you get down to business.'

Without a word Kezzie passed him the jar.

'Now,' said Owen, 'when did Miss Morgan take the sword?'

'In the night before May Day dawned,' said the queen. 'We were sitting here. All of a sudden the room grew so cold, so very cold. We thought it strange, but there can be frosts in May, so we lit a great fire in our bedchamber and . . . '

'And fell into a deep sleep,' said the king.

'Our dreams were bad,' said the queen.

'We rose early and uneasy,' said the king.

'And found the sword gone,' said the queen.

'She can't have gone far with it,' said Jack Dulac. 'We've seen her a lot since Will's birthday. Perhaps it's under her bed.'

'No,' said Will, 'Morgan le Fay would never hide Excalibur under her bed.'

'Long ago,' mused the king, 'long ago she threw my scabbard into a lake, the scabbard which shielded me from wounds. Long ago, long, long ago my sword came out of a lake, out of the clear pure waters. Perhaps she's thrown my sword into a lake, but into waters that are dirty and dark.'

'There aren't any lakes round here,' said Jack.

'But there are *ponds*,' said Will. 'The ponds we passed just now!'

'The ponds we flew over last night!' cried Lilah. 'The pond where Merlin dropped her . . . '

'The pond these frogs must go back to,' interrupted Merlin. 'Your tadpoles, Kezzie dear, before I count to ten, will all be frogs.'

'Ohh!' wailed Kezzie. 'Stop them, Merlin! Stop them!'

'No,' said Merlin. 'Magic's not for frittering. Magic is costly.'

'But we haven't got time to cope with Kezzie and her frogs now,' insisted Will.

'Why not?' said Jack.

'Indeed,' said the king. 'Why not?'

Kezzie's eyes filled with tears. She seized the king by the hand. 'Help me,' she begged. 'Come with me. Help me put the

little frogs back. It's so hard, so hard, every year, to have to put them back. Help me and I'll do anything for you, anything!'

And because the king was a true king, a great king, he said, 'But of course, Kezzie, of course I'll come with you. The sword must wait or the frogs will die. Will, please carry your sister's jar and I will carry her on my shoulders.'

Merlin handed the jar to Will and the king swung Kezzie up on to his shoulders. 'Lead on, Will' he commanded. 'Any real need must always be met. Remember that if you would be a knight.'

They made their way through the garden of gnarled apple trees with here a blossom, there a winter-bare twig, here a summer leaf and there an autumn apple as ripe as

85

Will's wish. It was a procession of past and present, of then and now: Will with the jar, the king and Kezzie, Lilah holding the queen's hand, Jack and Owen and, last, like a winged protector, Merlin in his feathered, starry cloak.

When they came to the shallow pond in the dips, the king put Kezzie down and Merlin held out the jar. 'Put them back,' he said sternly. 'You know you must.'

'I know,' said Kezzie sadly. 'But I always go with them.'

'Go with them, child?' said the queen.

'Go all the way with them,' explained Kezzie. 'Out into the middle of the pond.' She kicked off her shoes and pulled off her socks and took the jar from Merlin. She touched the king's hand and for a moment, sorrowing together, they stared out across the water.

'Help me be brave,' said Kezzie.

'Go, Kezzie,' said the king.

'Go, Kezzie,' called Merlin, swirling, dazzling, twinkling in his cloak, eyes fixed, trance-like, on the water.

Kezzie stepped into the pond and stopped. 'Ouch!' she cried. 'It's freezing.'

'The king is waiting,' called Merlin. 'The frogs are waiting.'

'You know if you don't put them back there won't be any next year,' said Will.

'I know, I know,' wailed Kezzie. 'Sometimes I wish I didn't know what I know . . . ' She splashed forlornly out into the pond, bent down and began to empty the jar into the larger, darker, muddier water.

'Good-bye,' she said. 'Good-bye, little frogs.' She stood a moment mourning over them.

'Come out now!' cried Will. 'You'll catch your death of cold.'

'They're not going!' called Kezzie. 'They're not going! They're sitting on something.' She peered down into the water. Then she looked up at the king. She looked as if she was going to burst with excitement. Her eyes sparkled, her cheeks went pale then pink but she could not speak.

'Come on, Kezzie,' groaned Will. 'Now what is it?'

'I . . . I . . . I've f . . . found it! I've found it!' she stuttered. 'No, *they've* found it!

The frogs have found the sword. They're all sitting on the sword!' She flung her arms wide towards the king. 'I have helped you,' she called. 'I have helped you. Come and see! Come!'

A great sigh rose up from all the companions at the pond's edge. The king stepped forward and strode through the waters. By the time he reached Kezzie she had gently pushed the little frogs away, and as the king lifted Excalibur from its murky hiding-place his face shone young, strong, astonished as it had on the day he drew the sword from its stone. Then he raised Excalibur high and waved it in an arc above his head so that the hilt seemed like a rainbow made of precious stones: ruby, emerald, sapphire, amethyst, topaz, amber and jacinth, all glowing with their own beauty, their own powers. And, holding Kezzie by the hand, he came back to them out of the waters and there, at once, the king knighted Will and Kezzie, Owen, Jack and Lilah.

'Kneel,' he ordered, the queen on his right, lovely, with her head held high as if she were wearing a crown; Merlin on his

left, dazzling, proud of his king, but restless, just a little restless.

'Kneel,' said the king. They knelt and he
tapped them one by one with the great
sword, lightly on each shoulder.

'Arise, Sir Will.'

'Arise, Sir Kezzie.'

'Arise, Sir Owen.'

'Arise, Sir Jack.'

'Arise, Sir Lilah.'

They rose, dazed and shaken.

And as they rose to their feet a cloud blew across the sun and the air went very cold. Crossing the cloud which covered the sun flew Miss Morgan; no longer the Miss Morgan they knew, but Morgan le Fay wrapped in white furs. Away she flew, not on a broomstick, but in a chariot encrusted with ice, pulled by a monstrous cat of dirty grey.

'She's given up,' smiled the king.

'She'll be off to those terrible sisters on their far, damp island,' said the queen.

'But you know Morgan,' said Merlin. 'Not for long and certainly not for ever. I'd best keep my eye on her.' He bowed to the king. 'My lord.' He bowed to the queen. 'My lady. All's well with you again.' And to the children he said, 'Knights, look after your king.' And he turned into a bird again. But not an owl for in daytime owls are at their sleepiest. He turned into an eagle. And as an eagle, sharp of eye, sharp of beak and with tireless wings, Merlin soared far and fast into the sky to watch over Morgan le Fay and to tell all other birds to keep their beady eyes on her and her wicked sisters on their far, damp island.

'I too must leave you for a time,' said the king. His voice was gentle but stern like a good father's. 'I have many things to watch over in many places, some near, some far.'

'But what shall we do?' said Owen.

'Go home,' said the king. 'Go home and do all the same things you did before Will made his wish to meet magic.'

'B . . . but . . . ,' stammered Jack and Will and Owen.

'Go home. You will find you have sharper ears, brighter eyes, noses for danger, legs that run faster and hands that aren't so clumsy. And, if I call you to me, and you can be sure that I will, I promise you will all hear me.'

He was their king. What could they do but bow and obey? You cannot say 'Good-bye' to your king.

Silently they turned towards home, but each time they looked back, the king still stood there, holding his great sword, its jewels ablaze, and the sky all red and gold behind him. The queen stood smiling at his side. Each time they looked back, which was often and often, the king and queen were still there until at long last they lost sight of them in the hilly dips and suddenly they could see the Crescent and their own houses.

On the last small hill they stopped to rest.

'Look at the hawthorn tree!' said Jack. 'Look how the light's caught it like a great flaming golden candle!'

'I can smell its flowers from here!' said Lilah.

'All spicy and sharp and hot, like summer,' said Kezzie.

'Isn't it beautiful?' said Owen.

'Beautiful,' said Will.